P9-BZP-058

THE GOLD COIN

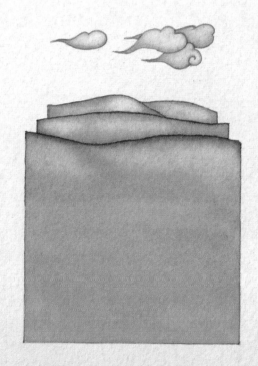

THE GOLD COIN

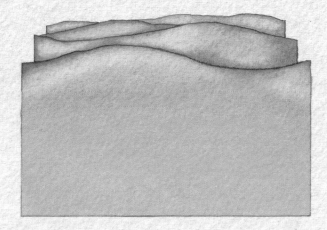

by Alma Flor Ada
illustrated by Neil Waldman

TRANSLATED FROM THE SPANISH BY BERNICE RANDALL

Aladdin Paperbacks

Aladdin Paperbacks
An imprint of Simon & Schuster
Children's Publishing Division
1230 Avenue of the Americas
New York, NY 10020

First Aladdin Paperbacks edition 1994
Manufactured in China
22 24 26 28 30 29 27 25 23 21
A hardcover edition of *The Gold Coin* is available from
Atheneum Books for Young Readers

Library of Congress Cataloging-in-Publication Data
Ada, Alma Flor
[Moneda de oro. English]
The gold coin/ by Alma Flor Ada ; illustrated by Neil
Waldman ; translated from the Spanish by Bernice Randall. –
1st Aladdin Books ed.
p.   cm.
Summary: Determined to steal an old woman's gold coin, a
young thief follows her all around the countryside and finds
himself involved in a series of unexpected activities.
ISBN 978-0-689-71793-2
[1. Stealing–Fiction.   2. Conduct of life–Fiction.   3. Central
America–Fiction.]   I. Waldman, Neil, ill.   II. Title.
PZ7.A1857Go   1994
[E]–dc20   93-14403

0711 SCP

To Rosalma, who believed this story
should reach all children, with gratitude
A. F. A.

For Jeremy, Eric,
and Lisa
N. W.

Juan had been a thief for many years. Because he did his stealing by night, his skin had become pale and sickly. Because he spent his time either hiding or sneaking about, his body had become shriveled and bent. And because he had neither friend nor relative to make him smile, his face was always twisted into an angry frown.

One night, drawn by a light shining through the trees, Juan came upon a hut. He crept up to the door and through a crack saw an old woman sitting at a plain, wooden table.

What was that shining in her hand? Juan wondered. He could not believe his eyes: It was a gold coin. Then he heard the woman say to herself, "I must be the richest person in the world."

Juan decided instantly that all the woman's gold must be his. He thought that the easiest thing to do was to watch until the woman left. Juan hid in the bushes and huddled under his poncho, waiting for the right moment to enter the hut.

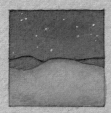

Juan was half asleep when he heard knocking at the door and the sound of insistent voices. A few minutes later, he saw the woman, wrapped in a black cloak, leave the hut with two men at her side.

Here's my chance! Juan thought. And, forcing open a window, he climbed into the empty hut.

He looked about eagerly for the gold. He looked under the bed. It wasn't there. He looked in the cupboard. It wasn't there, either. Where could it be? Close to despair, Juan tore away some beams supporting the thatch roof.

Finally, he gave up. There was simply no gold in the hut.

All I can do, he thought, is to find the old woman and make her tell me where she's hidden it.

So he set out along the path that she and her two companions had taken.

It was daylight by the time Juan reached the river. The countryside had been deserted, but here, along the riverbank, were two huts. Nearby, a man and his son were hard at work, hoeing potatoes.

It had been a long, long time since Juan had spoken to another human being. Yet his desire to find the woman was so strong that he went up to the farmers and asked, in a hoarse, raspy voice, "Have you seen a short, gray-haired woman, wearing a black cloak?"

"Oh, you must be looking for Doña Josefa," the young boy said. "Yes, we've seen her. We went to fetch her this morning, because my grandfather had another attack of—"

"Where is she now?" Juan broke in.

"She is long gone," said the father with a smile. "Some people from across the river came looking for her, because someone in their family is sick."

"How can I get across the river?" Juan asked anxiously.

"Only by boat," the boy answered. "We'll row you across later, if you'd like." Then turning back to his work, he added, "But first we must finish digging up the potatoes."

The thief muttered, "Thanks." But he quickly grew impatient. He grabbed a hoe and began to help the pair of farmers. The sooner we finish, the sooner we'll get across the river, he thought. And the sooner I'll get to my gold!

It was dusk when they finally laid down their hoes. The soil had been turned, and the wicker baskets were brimming with potatoes.

"Now can you row me across?" Juan asked the father anxiously.

"Certainly," the man said. "But let's eat supper first."

Juan had forgotten the taste of a home-cooked meal and the pleasure that comes from sharing it with others. As he sopped up the last of the stew with a chunk of dark bread, memories of other meals came back to him from far away and long ago.

By the light of the moon, father and son guided their boat across the river.

"What a wonderful healer Doña Josefa is!" the boy told Juan. "All she had to do to make Abuelo better was give him a cup of her special tea."

"Yes, and not only that," his father added, "she brought him a gold coin."

Juan was stunned. It was one thing for Doña Josefa to go around helping people. But how could she go around handing out gold coins—*his gold coins*?

When the threesome finally reached the other side of the river, they saw a young man sitting outside his hut.

"This fellow is looking for Doña Josefa," the father said, pointing to Juan.

"Oh, she left some time ago," the young man said.

"Where to?" Juan asked tensely.

"Over to the other side of the mountain," the young man replied, pointing to the vague outline of mountains in the night sky.

"How did she get there?" Juan asked, trying to hide his impatience.

"By horse," the young man answered. "They came on horseback to get her because someone had broken his leg."

"Well, then, I need a horse, too," Juan said urgently.

"Tomorrow," the young man replied softly. "Perhaps I can take you tomorrow, maybe the next day. First I must finish harvesting the corn."

So Juan spent the next day in the fields, bathed in sweat from sunup to sundown.

Yet each ear of corn that he picked seemed to bring him closer to his treasure. And later that evening, when he helped the young man husk several ears so they could boil them for supper, the yellow kernels glittered like gold coins.

While they were eating, Juan thought about Doña Josefa. Why, he wondered, would someone who said she was the world's richest woman spend her time taking care of every sick person for miles around?

The following day, the two set off at dawn. Juan could not recall when he last had noticed the beauty of the sunrise. He felt strangely moved by the sight of the mountains, barely lit by the faint rays of the morning sun.

As they neared the foothills, the young man said, "I'm not surprised you're looking for Doña Josefa. The whole countryside needs her. I went for her because my wife had been running a high fever. In no time at all, Doña Josefa had her on the road to recovery. And what's more, my friend, she brought her a gold coin!"

Juan groaned inwardly. To think that someone could hand out gold so freely! What a strange woman Doña Josefa is, Juan thought. Not only is she willing to help one person after another, but she doesn't mind traveling all over the countryside to do it!

"Well, my friend," said the young man finally, "this is where I must leave you. But you don't have far to walk. See that house over there? It belongs to the man who broke his leg."

The young man stretched out his hand to say good-bye. Juan stared at it for a moment. It had been a long, long time since the thief had shaken hands with anyone. Slowly, he pulled out a hand from under his poncho. When his companion grasped it firmly in his own, Juan felt suddenly warmed, as if by the rays of the sun.

But after he thanked the young man, Juan ran down the road. He was still eager to catch up with Doña Josefa. When he reached the house, a woman and a child were stepping down from a wagon.

"Have you seen Doña Josefa?" Juan asked.

"We've just taken her to Don Teodosio's," the woman said. "His wife is sick, you know—"

"How do I get there?" Juan broke in. "I've got to see her."

"It's too far to walk," the woman said amiably. "If you'd like, I'll take you there tomorrow. But first I must gather my squash and beans."

So Juan spent yet another long day in the fields. Working beneath the summer sun, Juan noticed that his skin had begun to tan. And although he had to stoop down to pick the squash, he found that he could now stretch his body. His back had begun to straighten, too.

Later, when the little girl took him by the hand to show him a family of rabbits burrowed under a fallen tree, Juan's face broke into a smile. It had been a long, long time since Juan had smiled.

Yet his thoughts kept coming back to the gold.

The following day, the wagon carrying Juan and the woman lumbered along a road lined with coffee fields.

The woman said, "I don't know what we would have done without Doña Josefa. I sent my daughter to our neighbor's house, who then brought Doña Josefa on horseback. She set my husband's leg and then showed me how to brew a special tea to lessen the pain."

Getting no reply, she went on. "And, as if that weren't enough, she brought him a gold coin. Can you imagine such a thing?"

Juan could only sigh. No doubt about it, he thought, Doña Josefa is someone special. But Juan didn't know whether to be happy that Doña Josefa had so much gold she could freely hand it out, or angry for her having already given so much of it away.

When they finally reached Don Teodosio's house, Doña Josefa was already gone. But here, too, there was work that needed to be done....

Juan stayed to help with the coffee harvest. As he picked the red berries, he gazed up from time to time at the trees that grew, row upon row, along the hillsides. What a calm, peaceful place this is! he thought.

The next morning, Juan was up at daybreak. Bathed in the soft, dawn light, the mountains seemed to smile at him. When Don Teodosio offered him a lift on horseback, Juan found it difficult to have to say good-bye.

"What a good woman Doña Josefa is!" Don Teodosio said, as they rode down the hill toward the sugarcane fields. "The minute she heard about my wife being sick, she came with her special herbs. And as if that weren't enough, she brought my wife a gold coin!"

In the stifling heat, the kind that often signals the approach of a storm, Juan simply sighed and mopped his brow. The pair continued riding for several hours in silence.

Juan then realized he was back in familiar territory, for they were now on the stretch of road he had traveled only a week ago—though how much longer it now seemed to him. He jumped off Don Teodosio's horse and broke into a run.

This time the gold would not escape him! But he had to move quickly, so he could find shelter before the storm broke.

Out of breath, Juan finally reached Doña Josefa's hut. She was standing by the door, shaking her head slowly as she surveyed the ransacked house.

"So I've caught up with you at last!" Juan shouted, startling the old woman. "Where's the gold?"

"The gold coin?" Doña Josefa said, surprised and looking at Juan intently. "Have you come for the gold coin? I've been trying hard to give it to someone who might need it," Doña Josefa said. "First to an old man who had just gotten over a bad attack. Then to a young woman who had been running a fever. Then to a man with a broken leg. And finally to Don Teodosio's wife. But none of them would take it. They all said, 'Keep it. There must be someone who needs it more.'"

Juan did not say a word.

"You must be the one who needs it," Doña Josefa said.

She took the coin out of her pocket and handed it to him. Juan stared at the coin, speechless.

At that moment a young girl appeared, her long braid bouncing as she ran. "Hurry, Doña Josefa, please!" she said breathlessly. "My mother is all alone, and the baby is due any minute."

"Of course, dear," Doña Josefa replied. But as she glanced up at the sky, she saw nothing but black clouds. The storm was nearly upon them. Doña Josefa sighed deeply.

"But how can I leave now? Look at my house! I don't know what has happened to the roof. The storm will wash the whole place away!"

And there was a deep sadness in her voice.

Juan took in the child's frightened eyes, Doña Josefa's sad, distressed face, and the ransacked hut.

"Go ahead, Doña Josefa," he said. "Don't worry about your house. I'll see that the roof is back in shape, good as new."

The woman nodded gratefully, drew her cloak
about her shoulders, and took the child by the hand.
As she turned to leave, Juan held out his hand.
    "Here, take this," he said, giving her the gold coin.
"I'm sure the newborn will need it more than I."